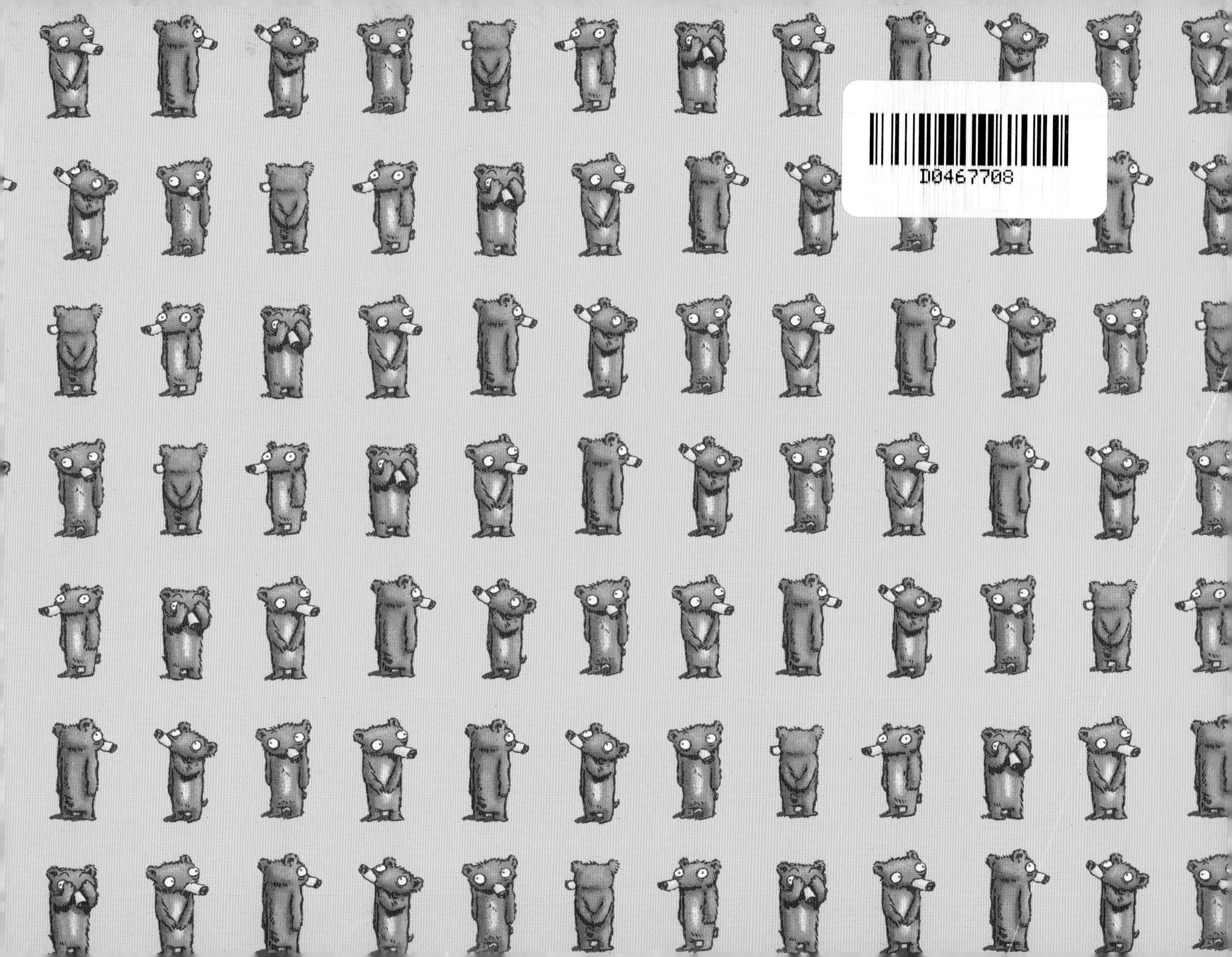

GOLDILOCKS AND THE SEVEN SQUAT BEARS
ÉMILE BRAVO

Translation: J. Gustave McBride

First published in France under the title: *Boucle d'or et les sept ours nains*
© Editions du Seuil, 2004

English translation © 2010 by Hachette Book Group, Inc.

Yen Press
Hachette Book Group
237 Park Avenue, New York, NY 10017

www.HachetteBookGroup.com
www.YenPress.com

Yen Press is an imprint of Hachette Book Group, Inc.
The Yen Press name and logo are trademarks of Hachette Book Group, Inc.

First Yen Press Edition: August 2010

ISBN: 978-0-316-08358-4

Library of Congress Control Number: 2009943851

10 9 8 7 6 5 4 3 2 1

SC

Printed in China

GOLDILOCKS
AND THE
SEVEN
SQUAT
BEARS

ÉMILE BRAVO

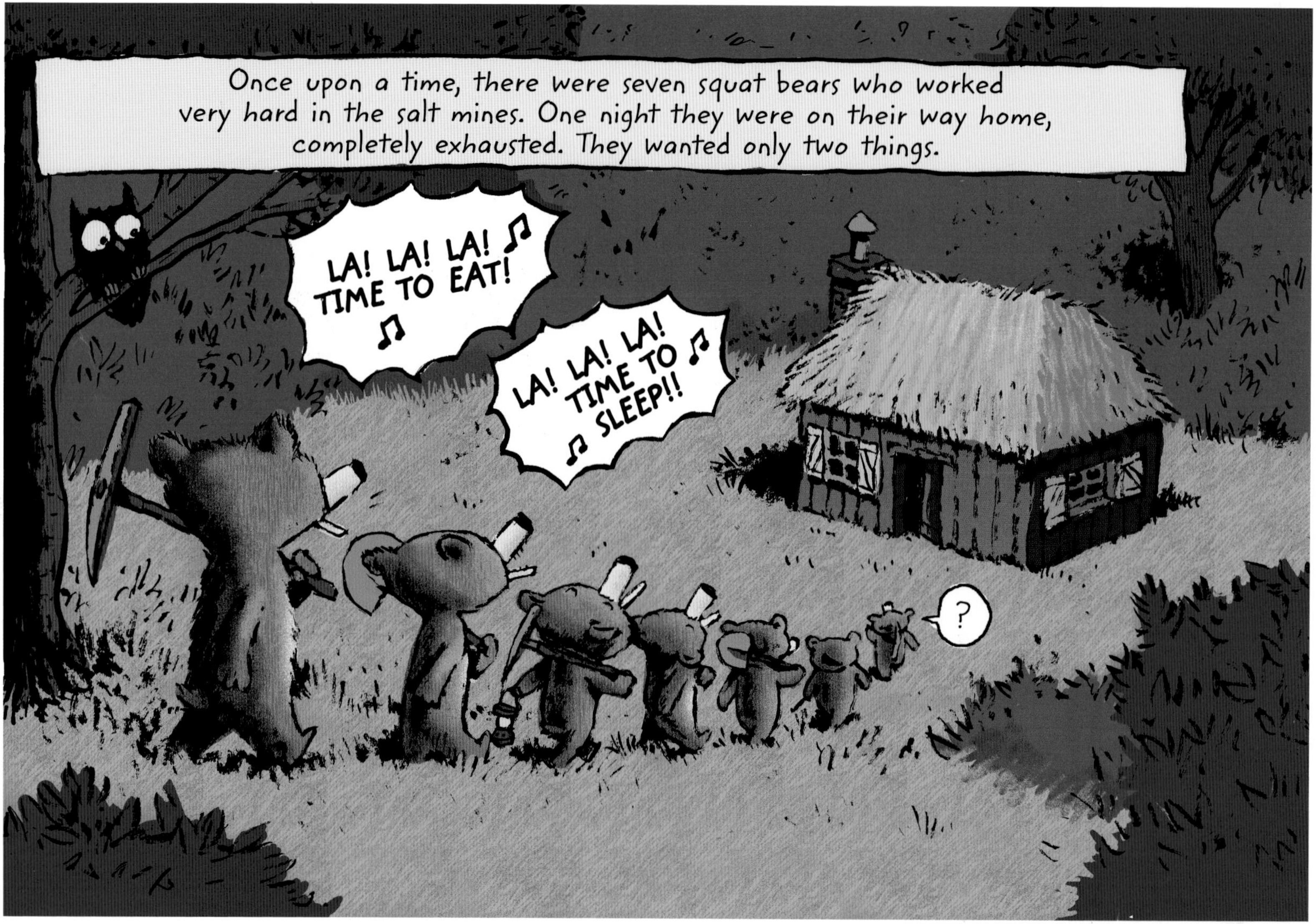
Once upon a time, there were seven squat bears who worked very hard in the salt mines. One night they were on their way home, completely exhausted. They wanted only two things.
LA! LA! LA! ♫ TIME TO EAT! ♫
LA! LA! LA! TIME TO ♫ ♫ SLEEP!!
?

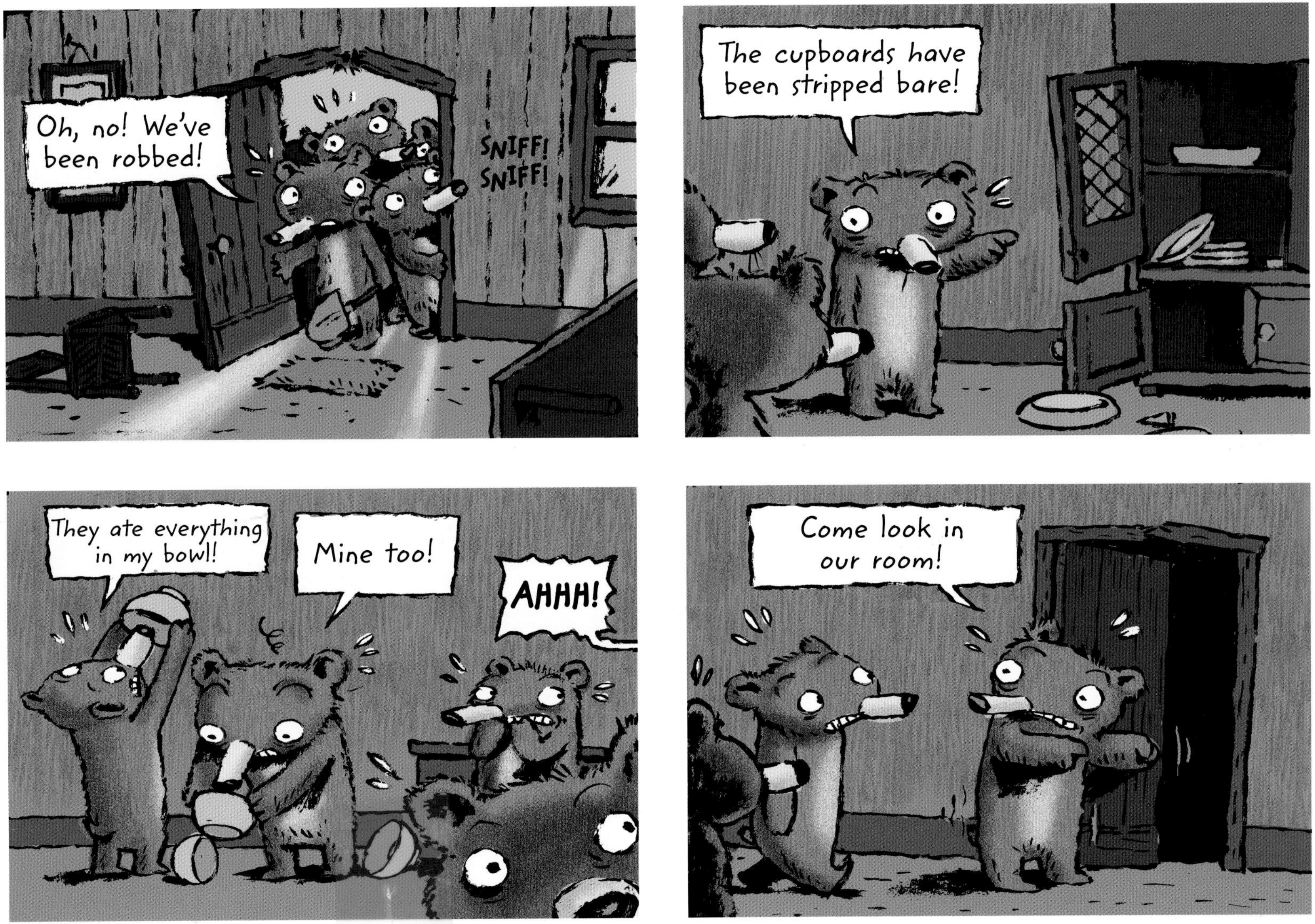
Oh, no! We've been robbed!
SNIFF! SNIFF!
The cupboards have been stripped bare!
They ate everything in my bowl!
Mine too!
AHHH!
Come look in our room!

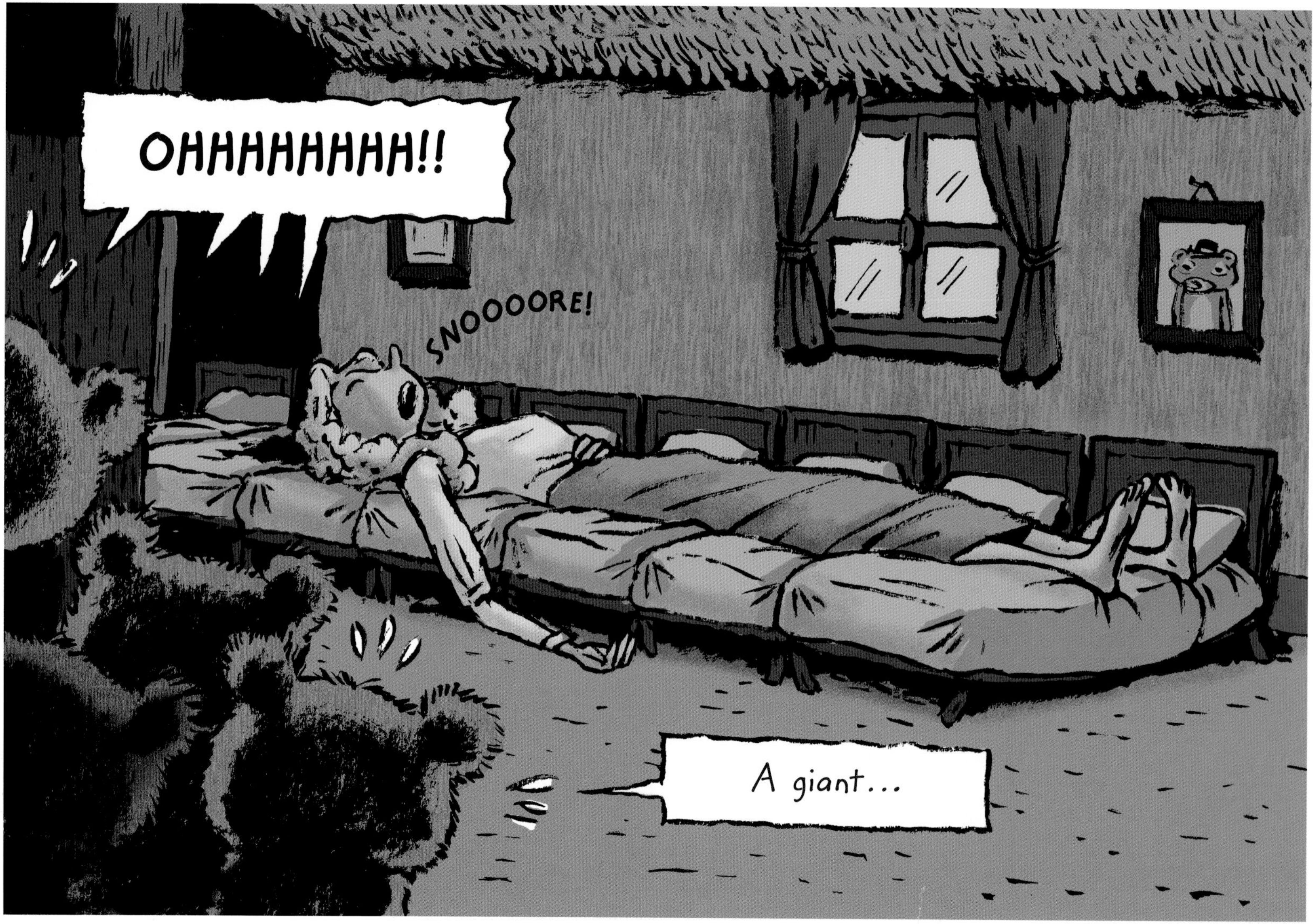
OHHHHHHHH!!
SNOOOORE!
A giant...

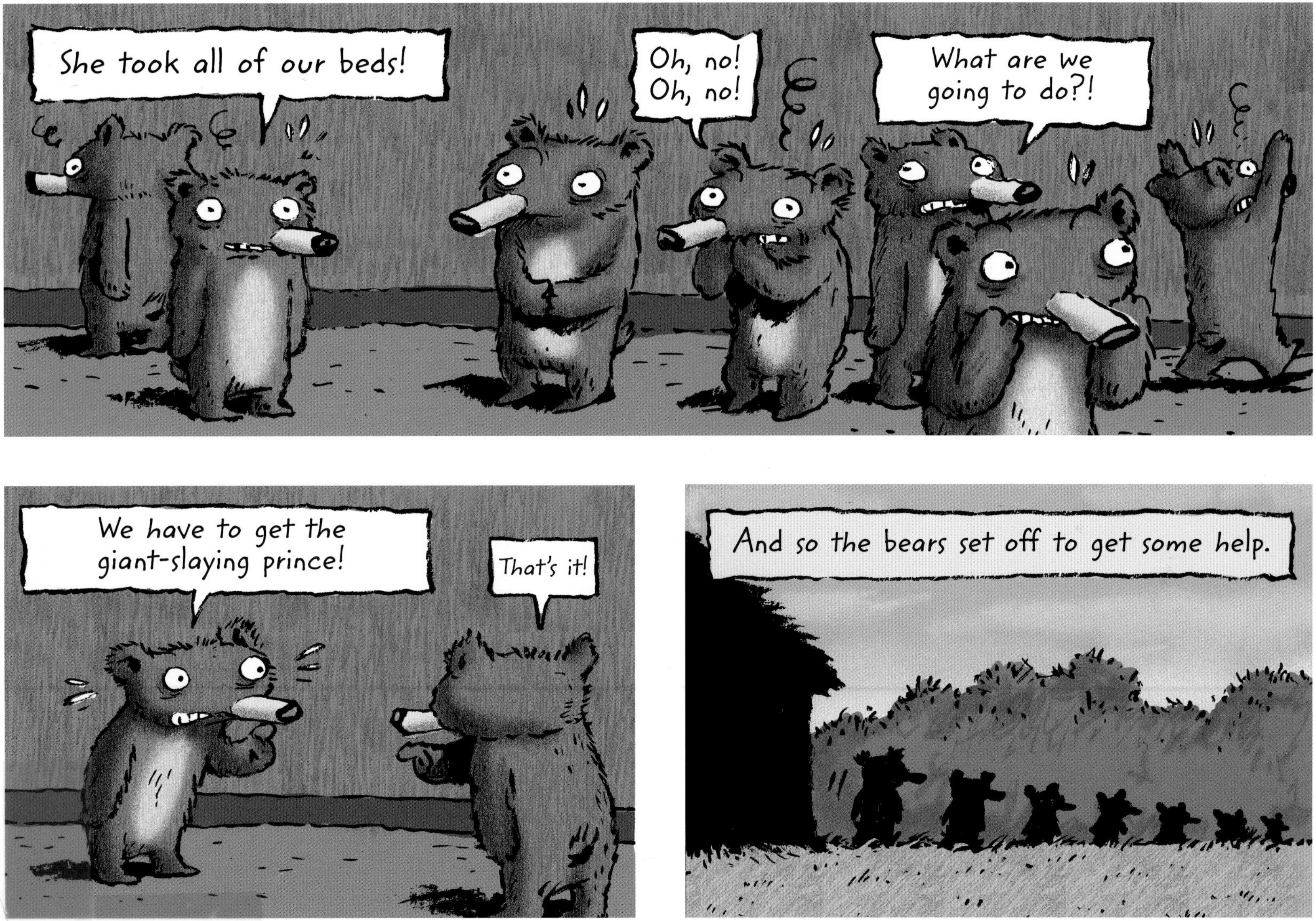
She took all of our beds!
Oh, no! Oh, no!
What are we going to do?!
We have to get the giant-slaying prince!
That's it!
And so the bears set off to get some help.

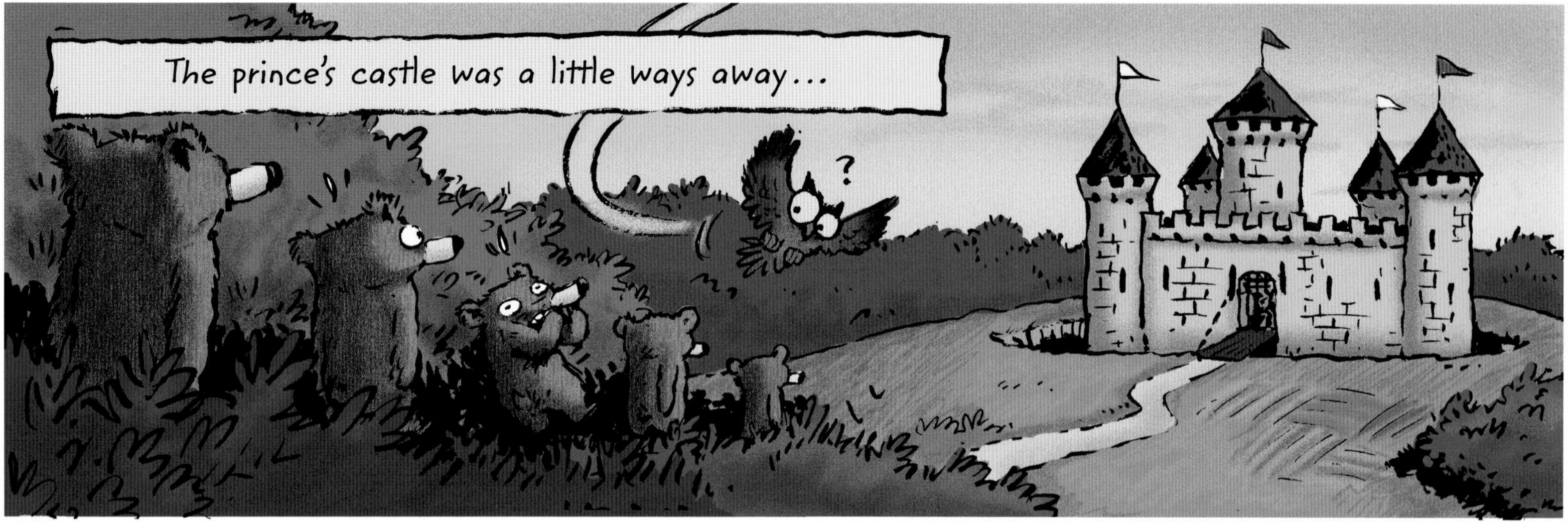
The prince's castle was a little ways away...
?

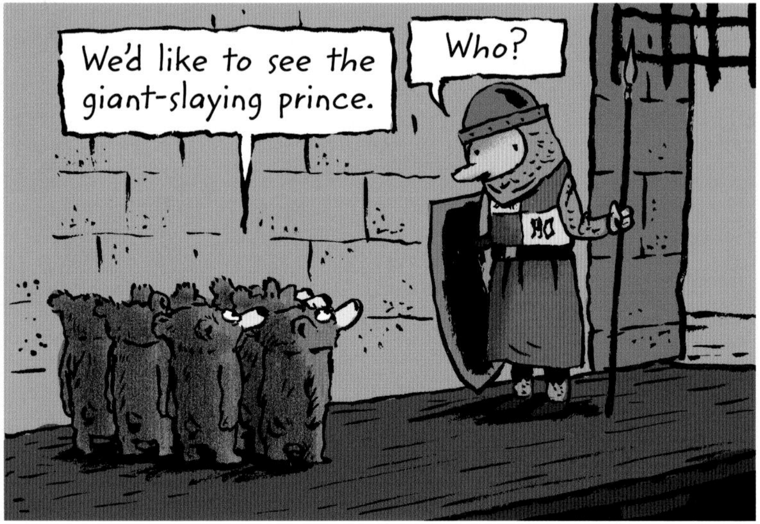
We'd like to see the giant-slaying prince.
Who?

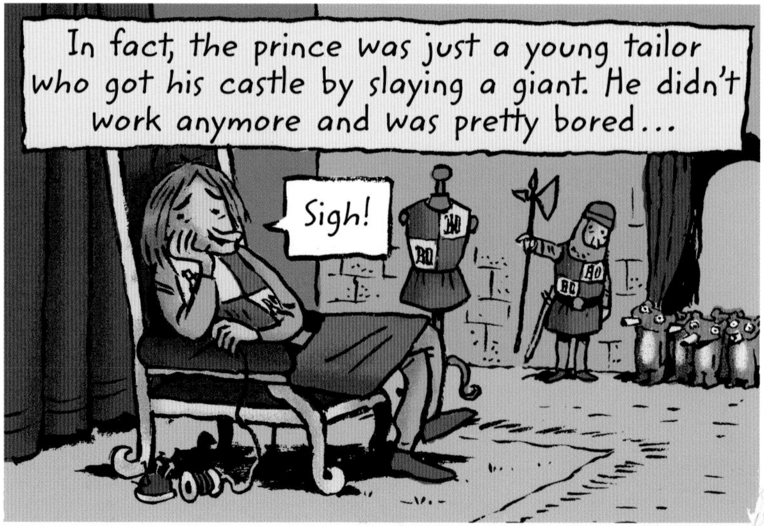
In fact, the prince was just a young tailor who got his castle by slaying a giant. He didn't work anymore and was pretty bored...
Sigh!

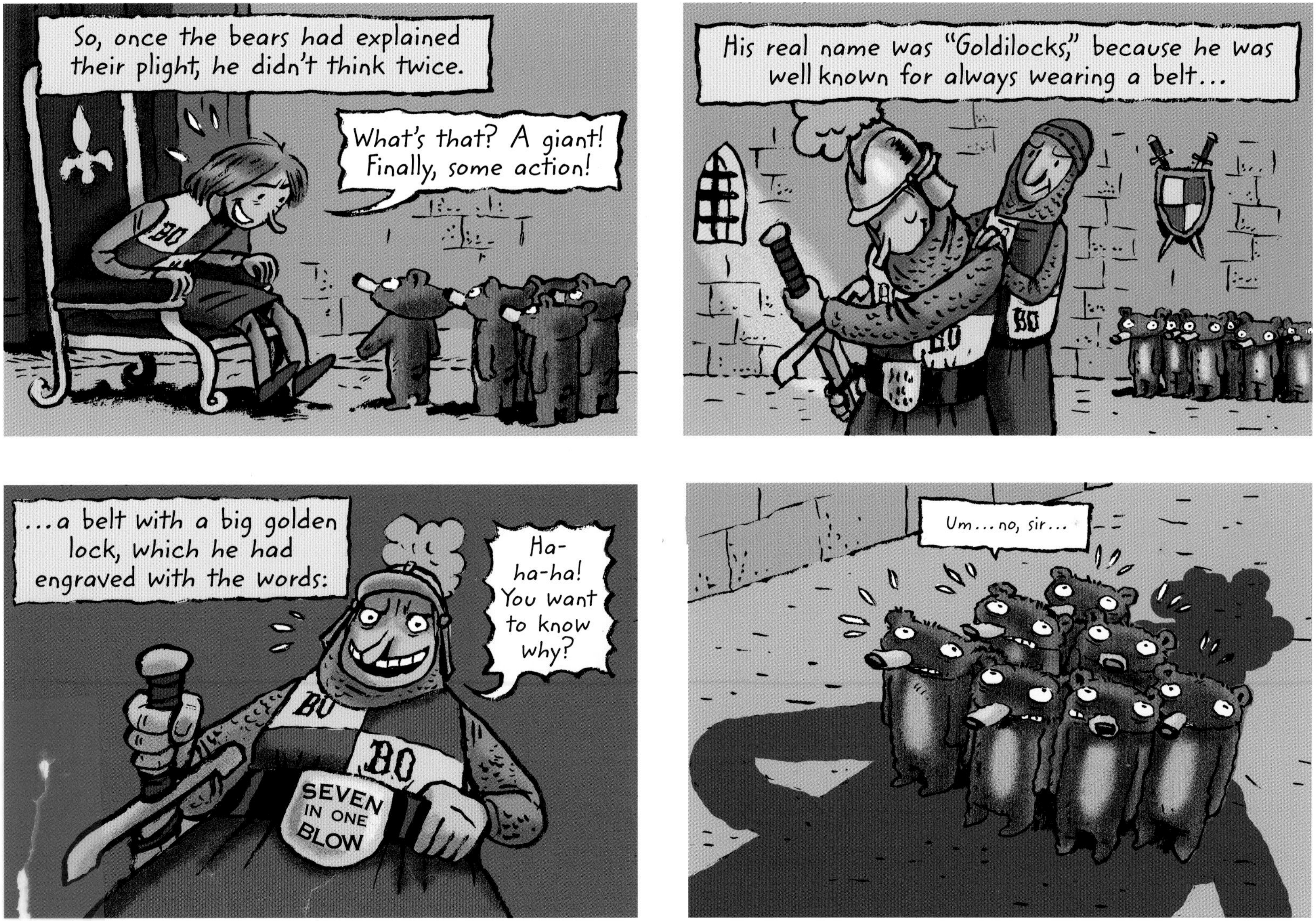
So, once the bears had explained their plight, he didn't think twice.
What's that? A giant! Finally, some action!
His real name was "Goldilocks," because he was well known for always wearing a belt...
...a belt with a big golden lock, which he had engraved with the words:
SEVEN IN ONE BLOW
Ha-ha-ha! You want to know why?
Um... no, sir...

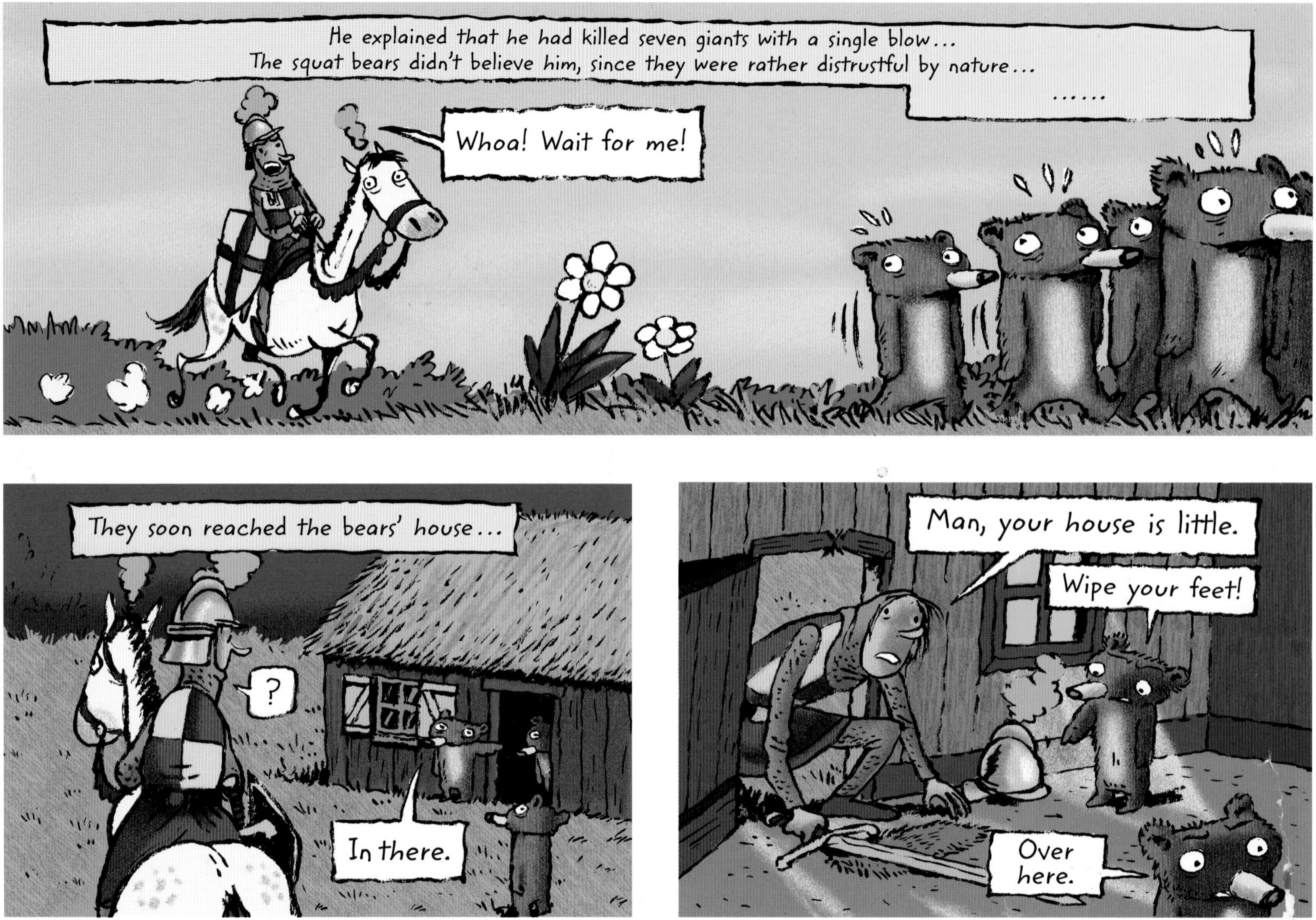
He explained that he had killed seven giants with a single blow...
The squat bears didn't believe him, since they were rather distrustful by nature...
......
Whoa! Wait for me!
They soon reached the bears' house...
?
In there.
Man, your house is little.
Wipe your feet!
Over here.

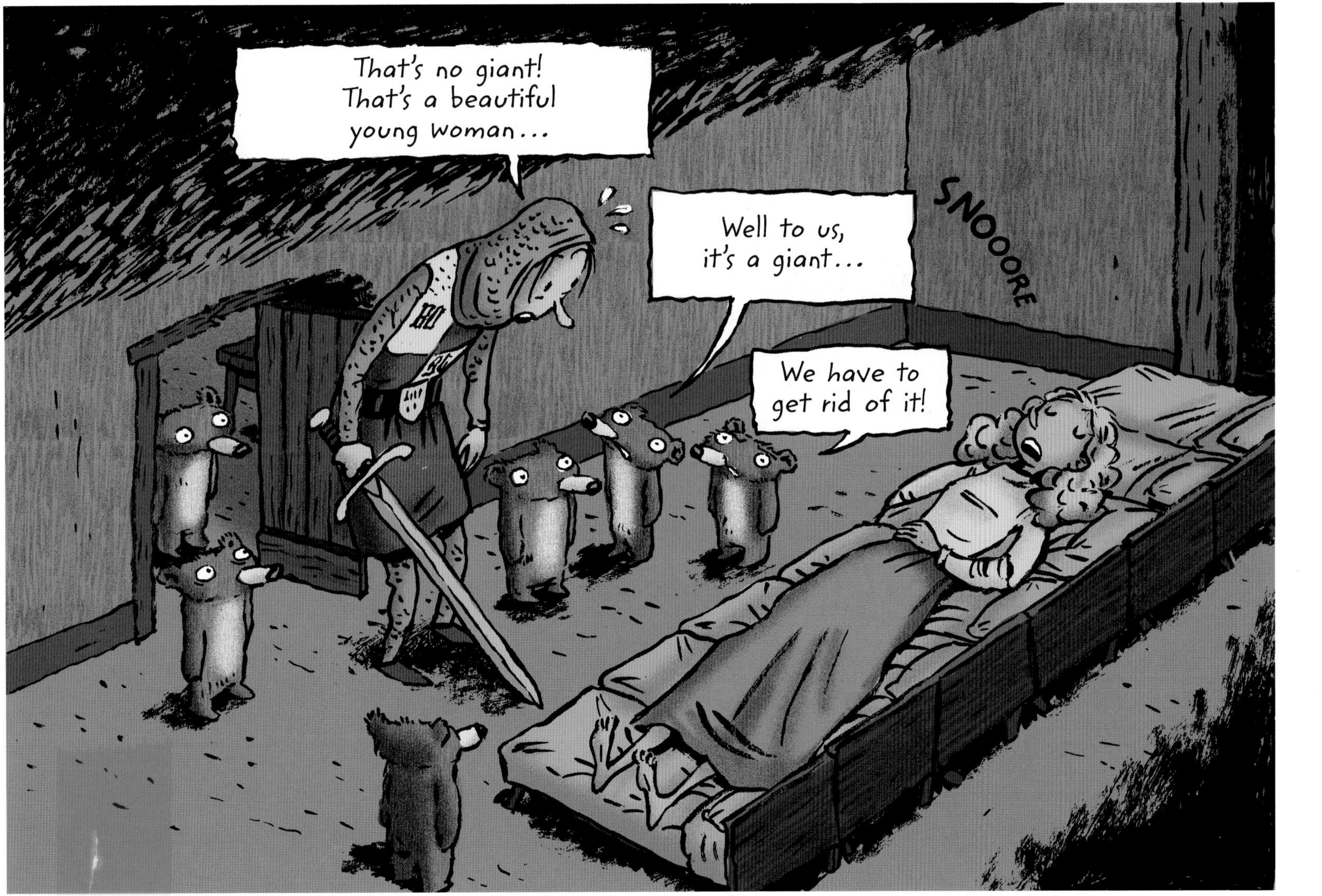
That's no giant! That's a beautiful young woman...
Well to us, it's a giant...
We have to get rid of it!
SNOOORE

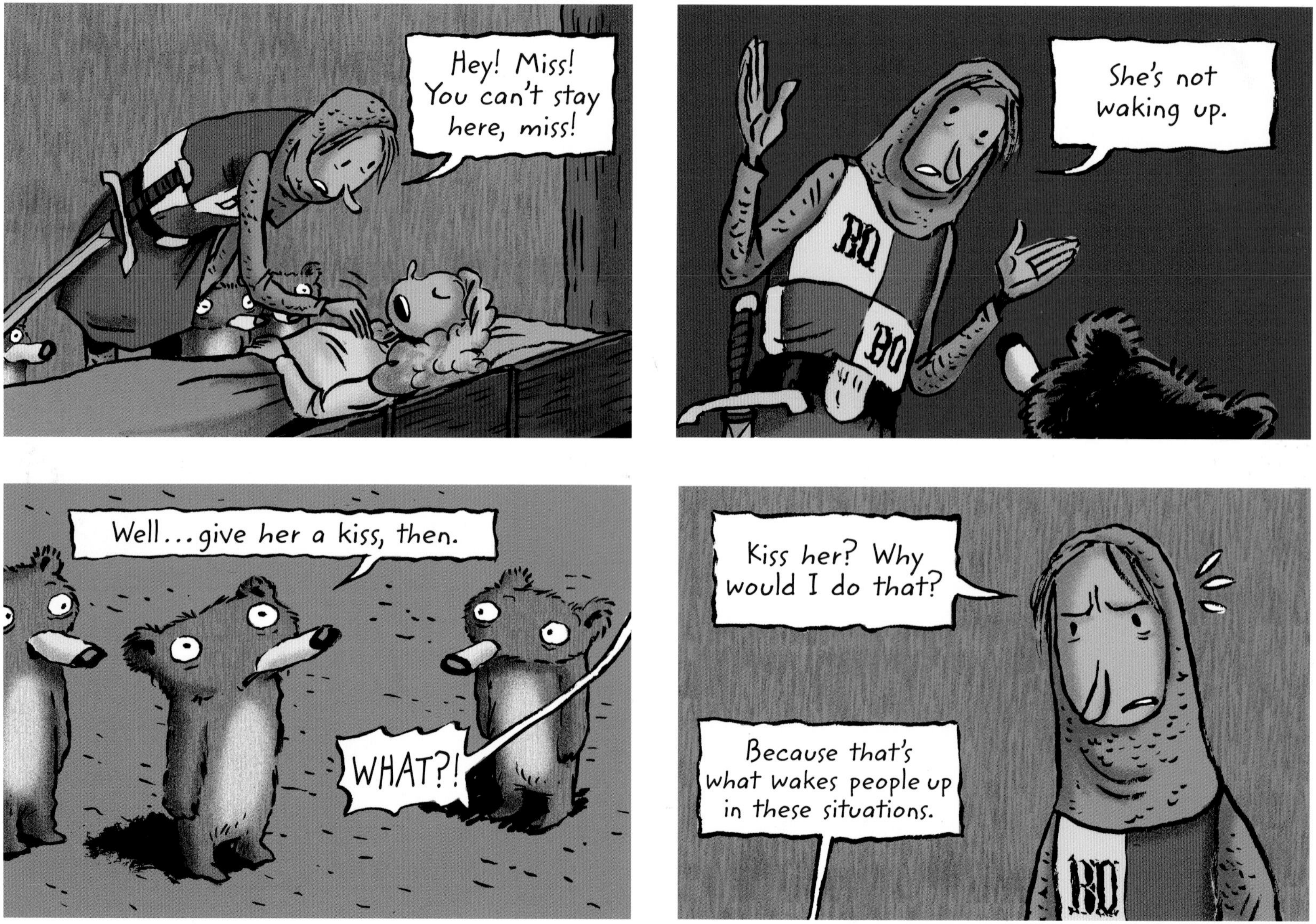
Hey! Miss! You can't stay here, miss!
She's not waking up.
Well... give her a kiss, then.
WHAT?!
Kiss her? Why would I do that?
Because that's what wakes people up in these situations.

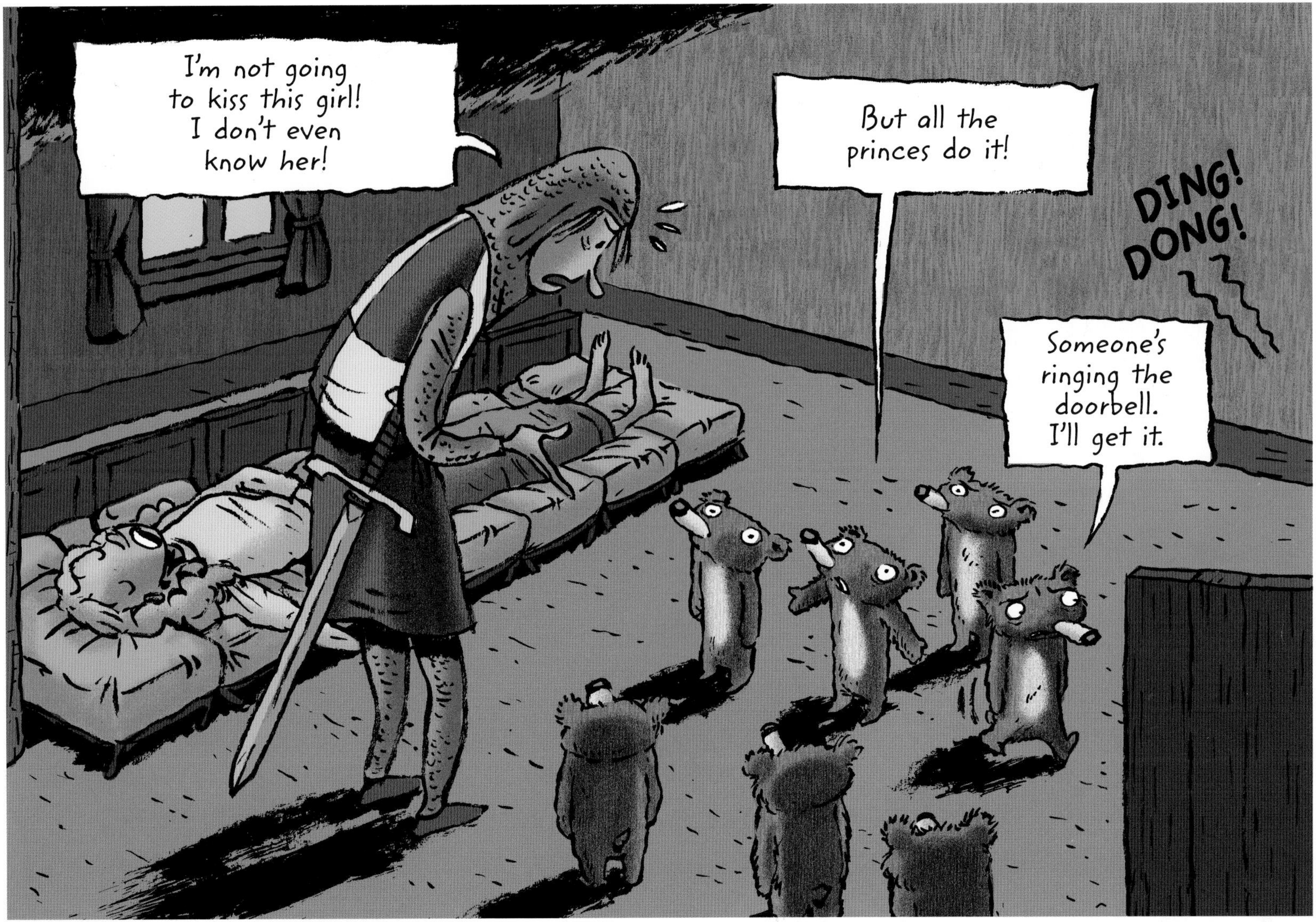
I'm not going to kiss this girl! I don't even know her!
But all the princes do it!
DING! DONG!
Someone's ringing the doorbell. I'll get it.

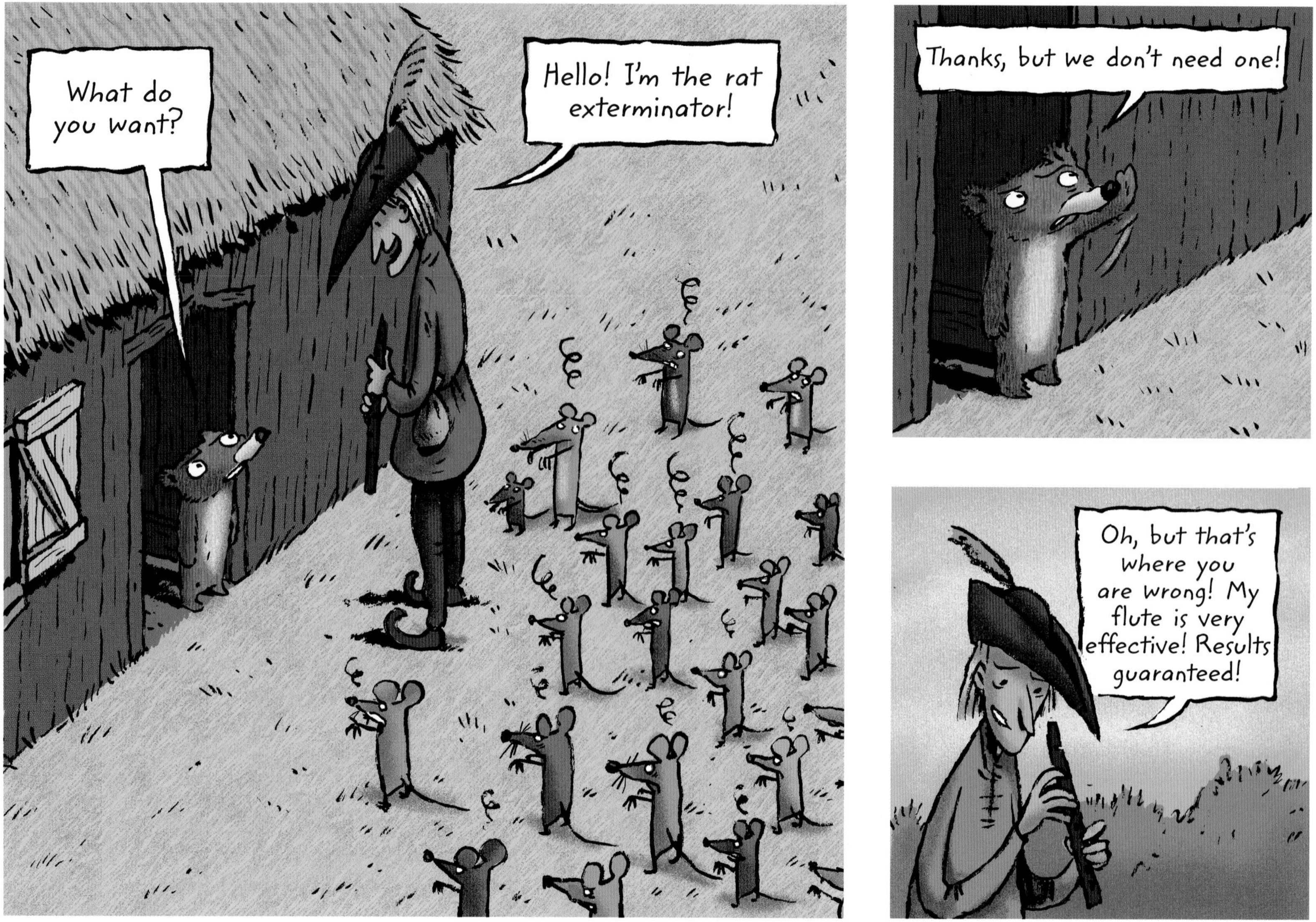
What do you want?
Hello! I'm the rat exterminator!
Thanks, but we don't need one!
Oh, but that's where you are wrong! My flute is very effective! Results guaranteed!

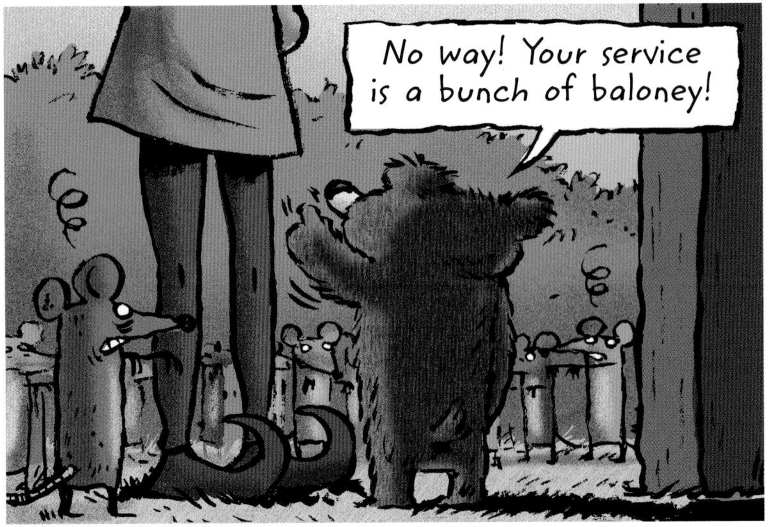
No way! Your service is a bunch of baloney!

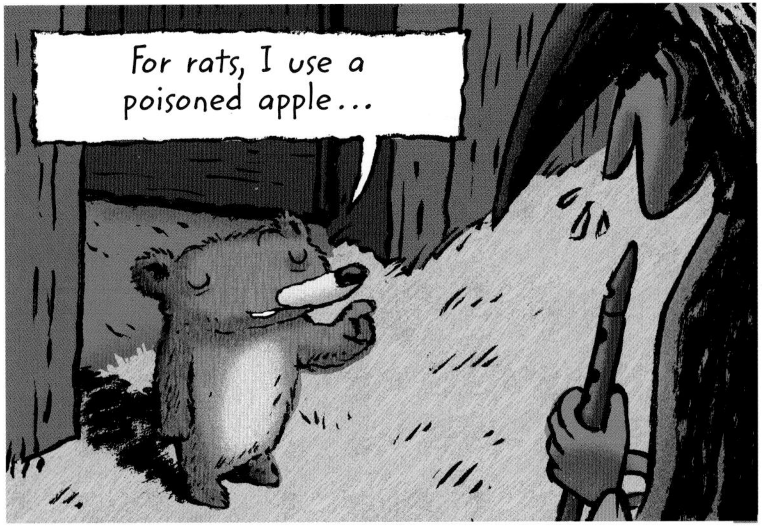
For rats, I use a poisoned apple...

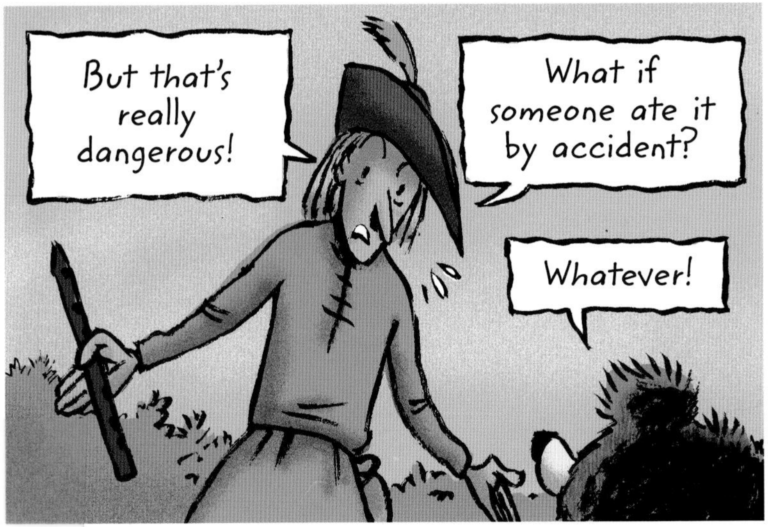
But that's really dangerous!
What if someone ate it by accident?
Whatever!

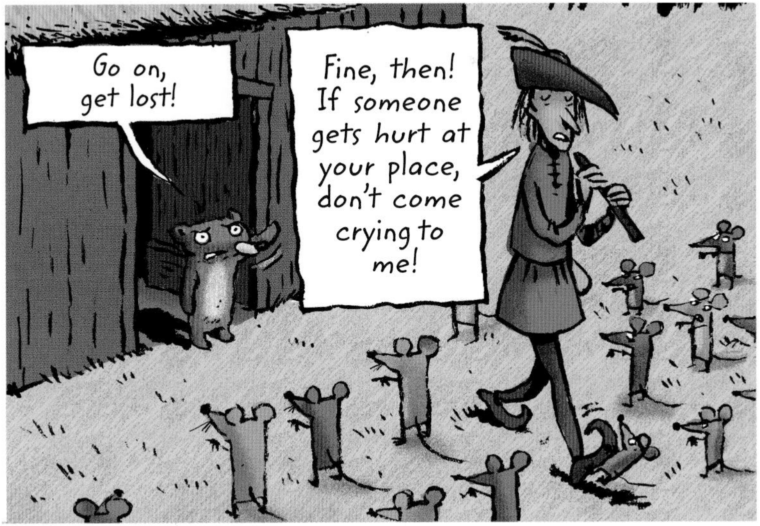
Go on, get lost!
Fine, then! If someone gets hurt at your place, don't come crying to me!

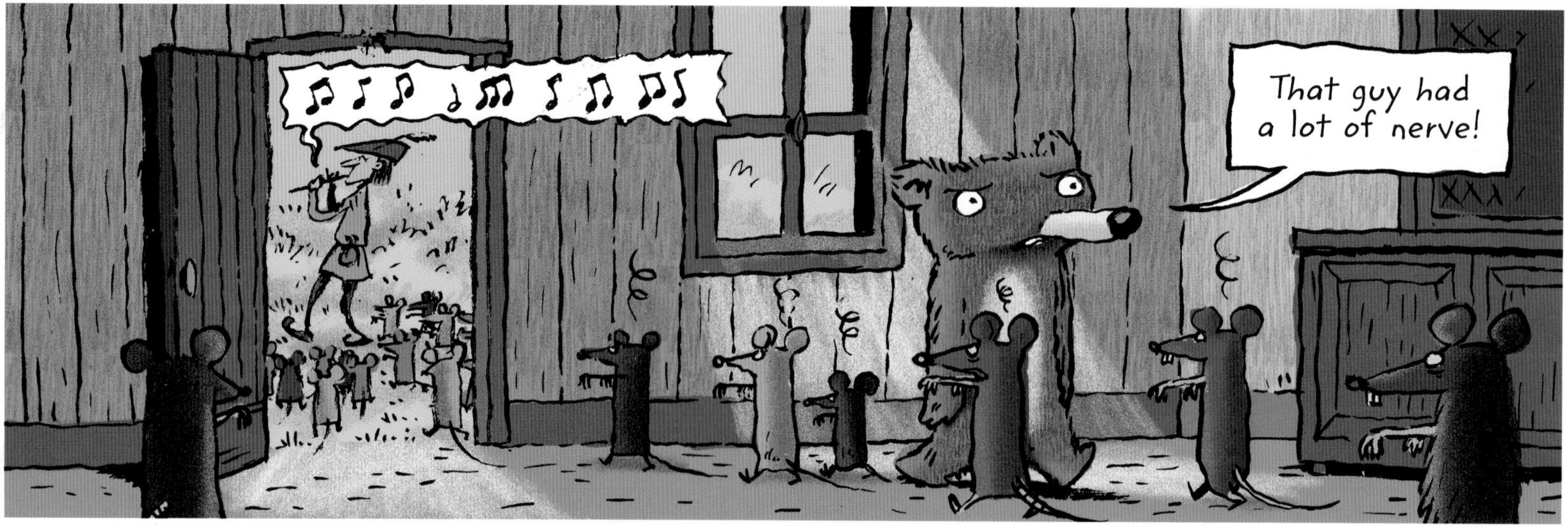
That guy had a lot of nerve!

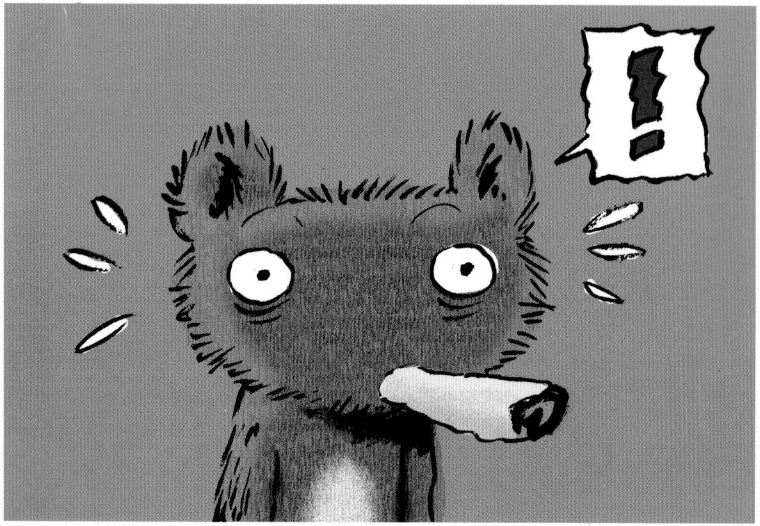
!

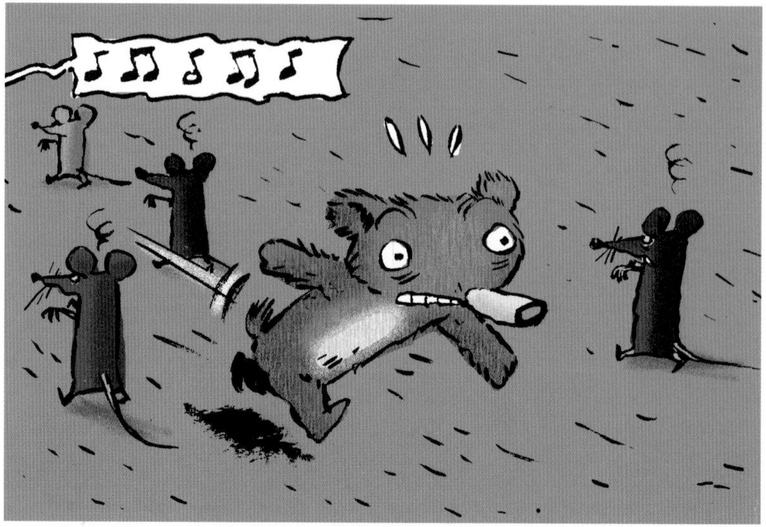

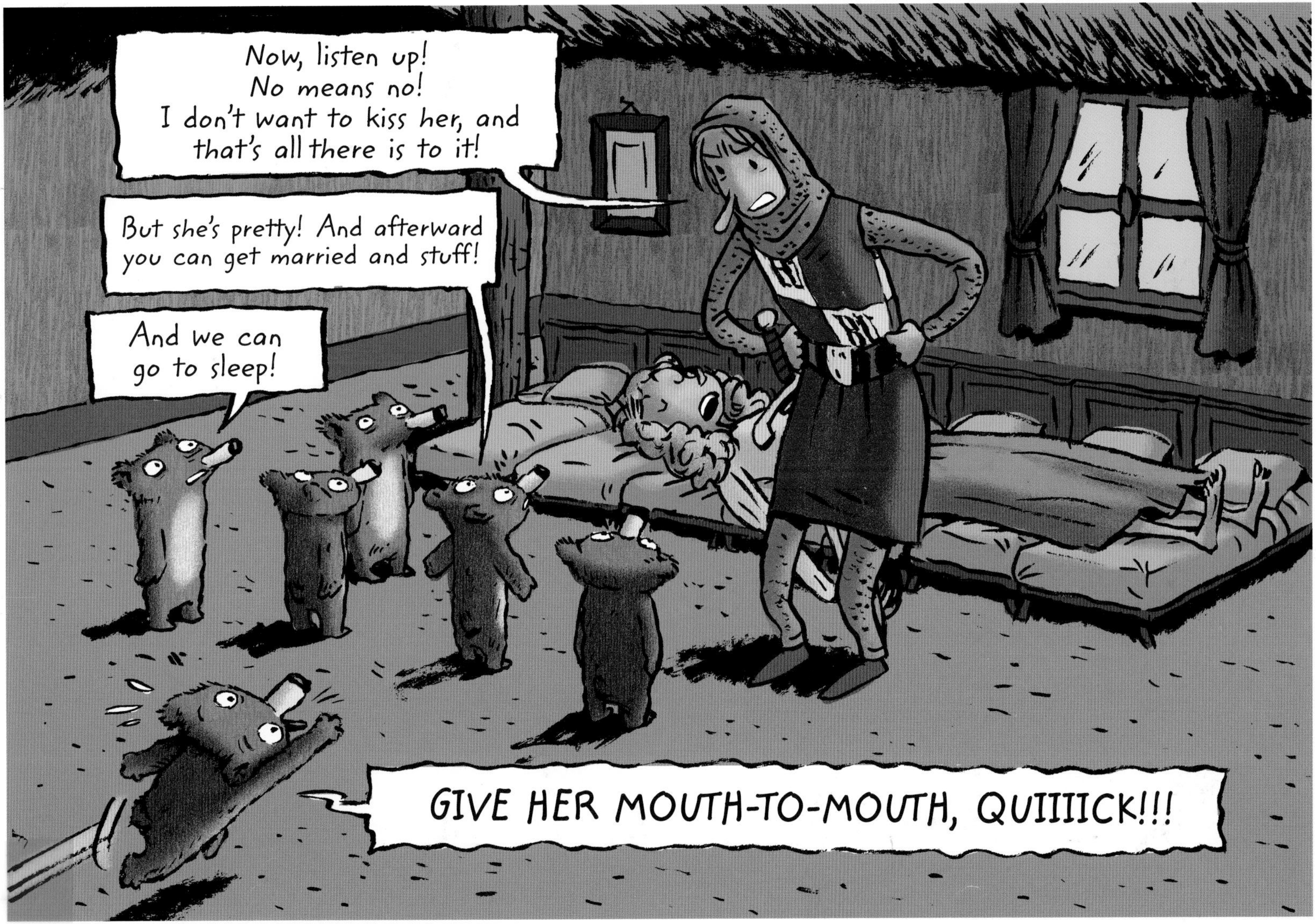
Now, listen up! No means no! I don't want to kiss her, and that's all there is to it!
But she's pretty! And afterward you can get married and stuff!
And we can go to sleep!
GIVE HER MOUTH-TO-MOUTH, QUIIIICK!!!

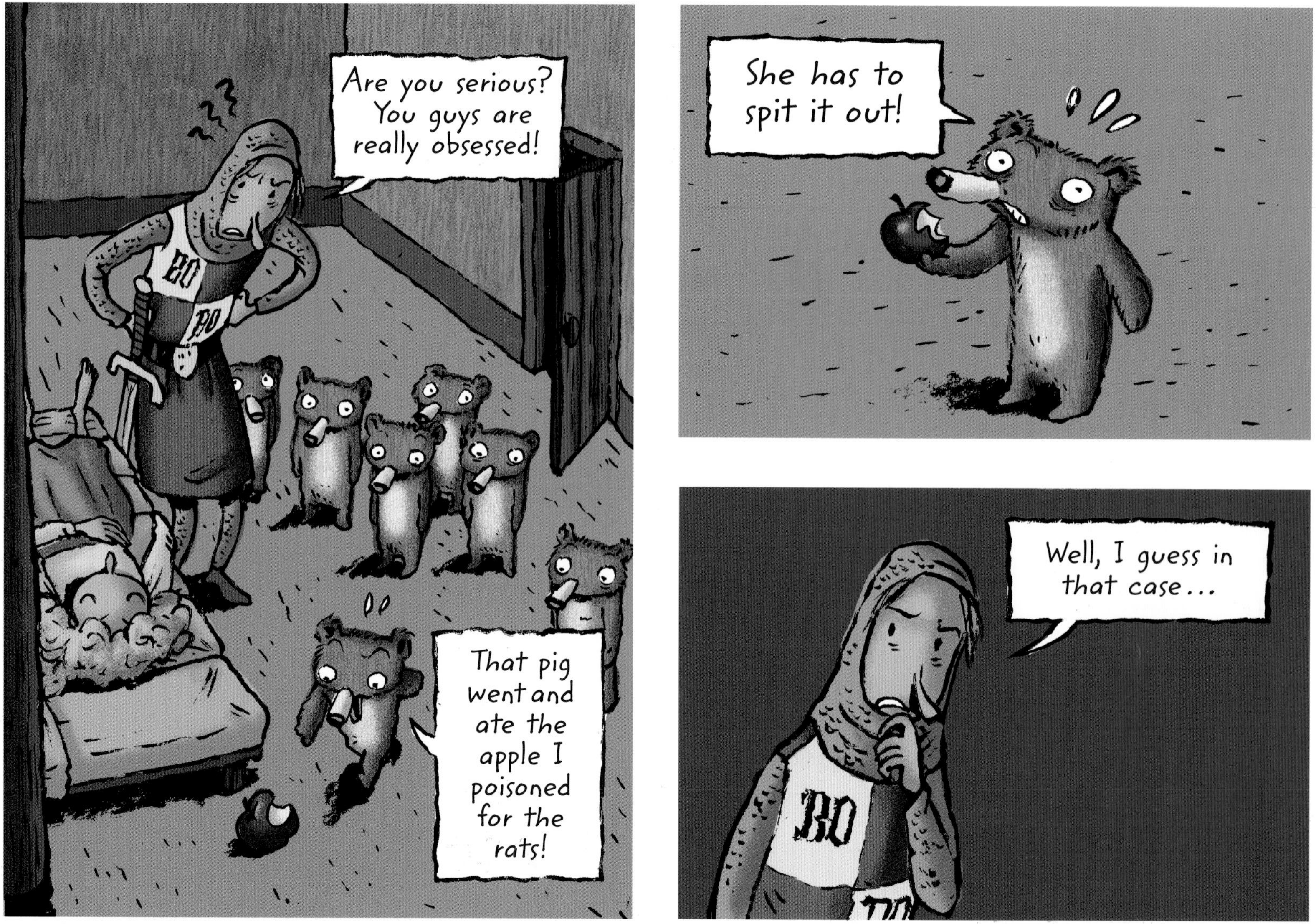
Are you serious? You guys are really obsessed!
That pig went and ate the apple I poisoned for the rats!
She has to spit it out!
Well, I guess in that case...

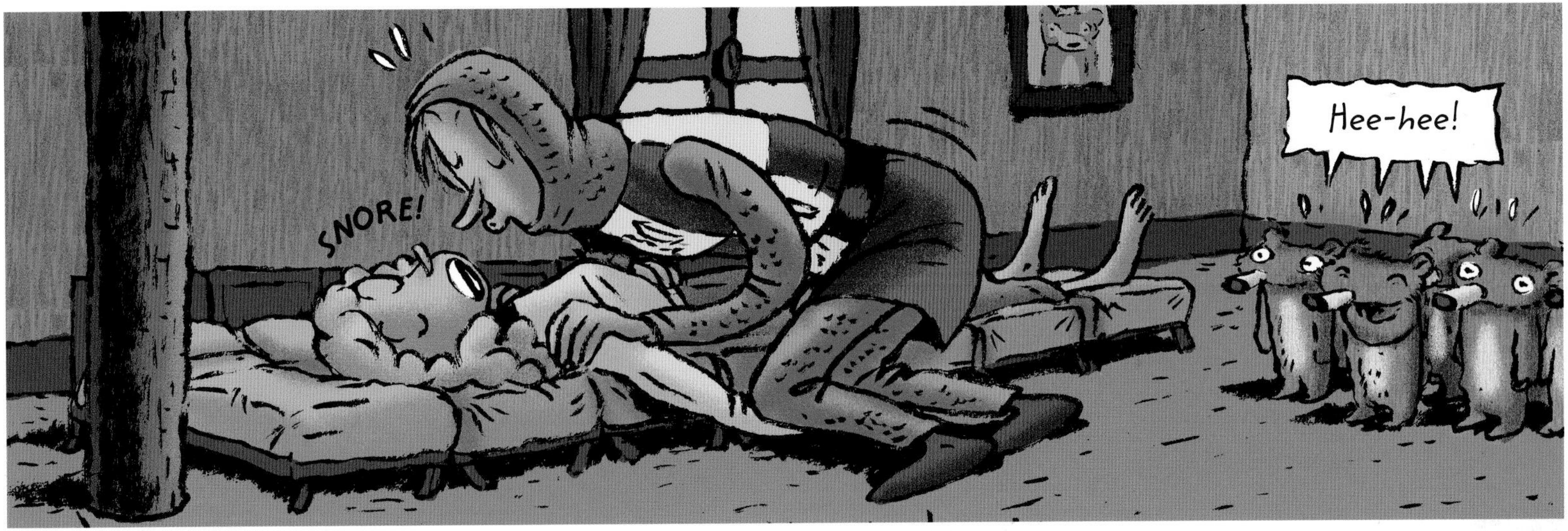
SNORE!
Hee-hee!

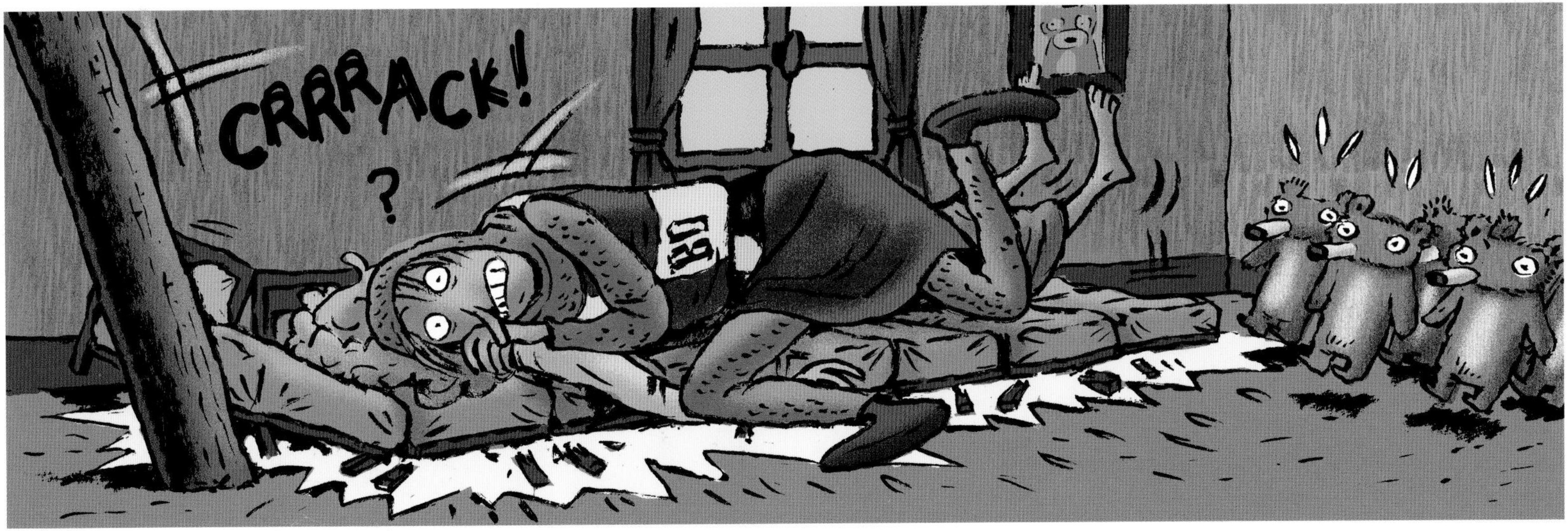
CRRRACK!
?

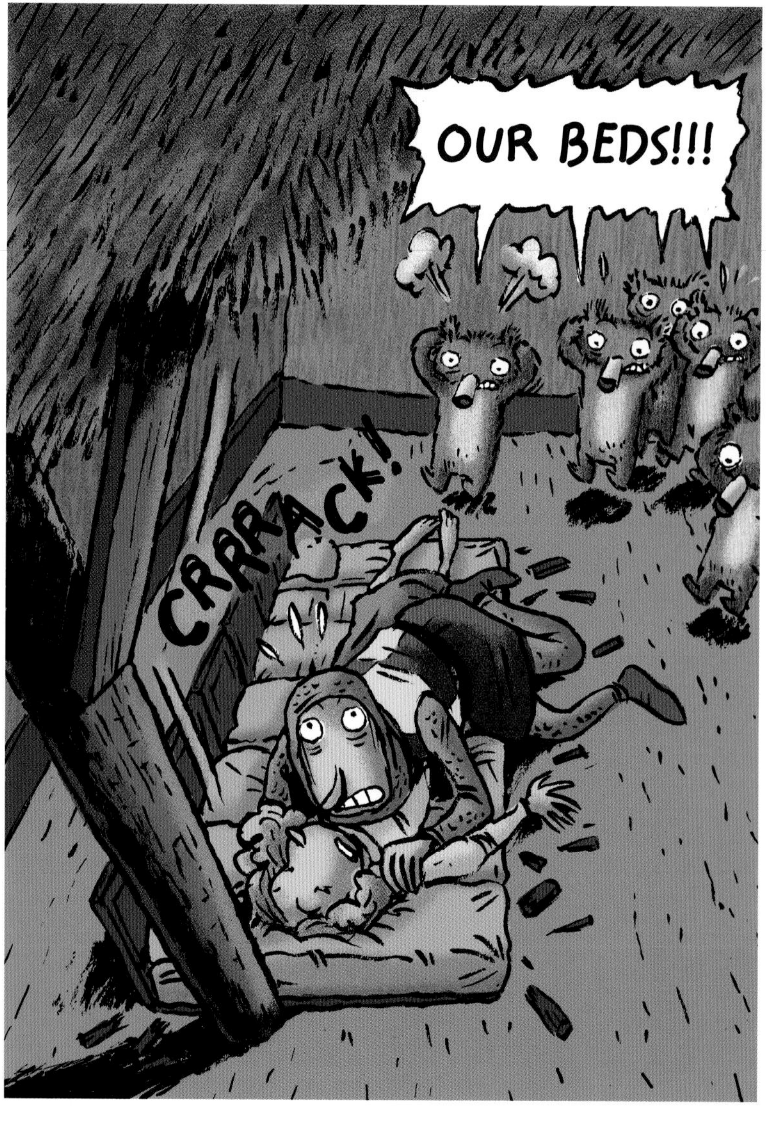
OUR BEDS!!!
CRRRACK!
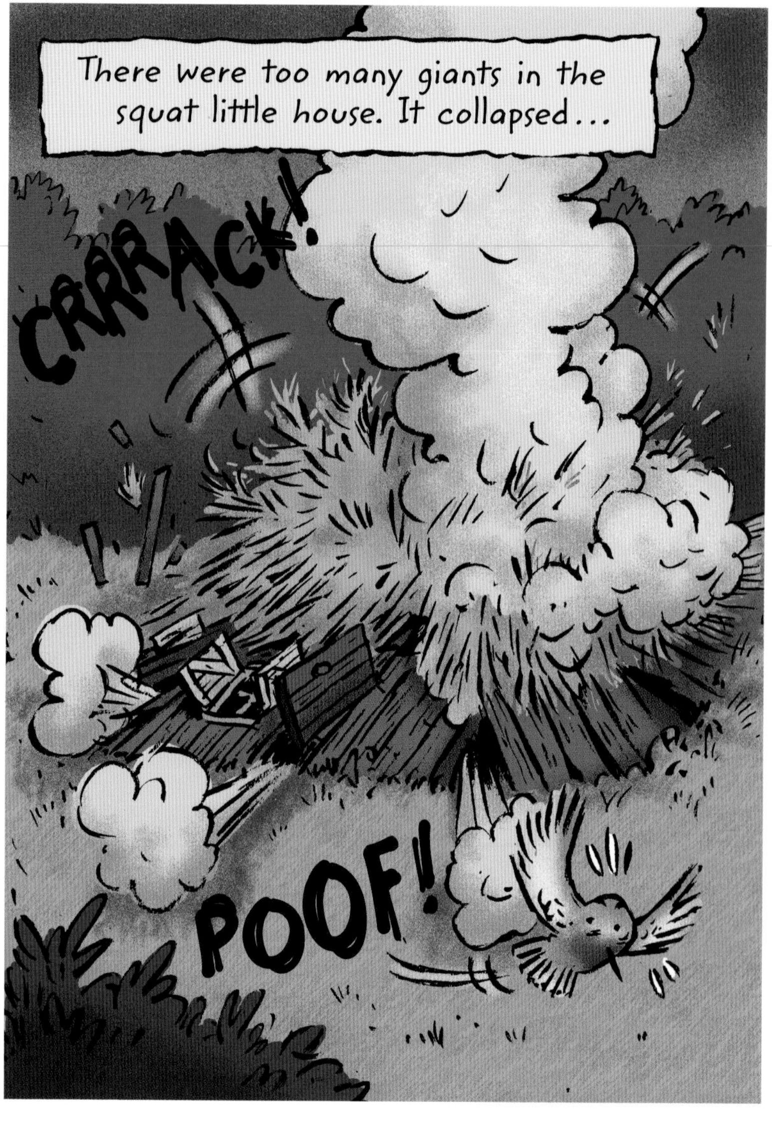
There were too many giants in the squat little house. It collapsed...
CRRRACK!
POOF!

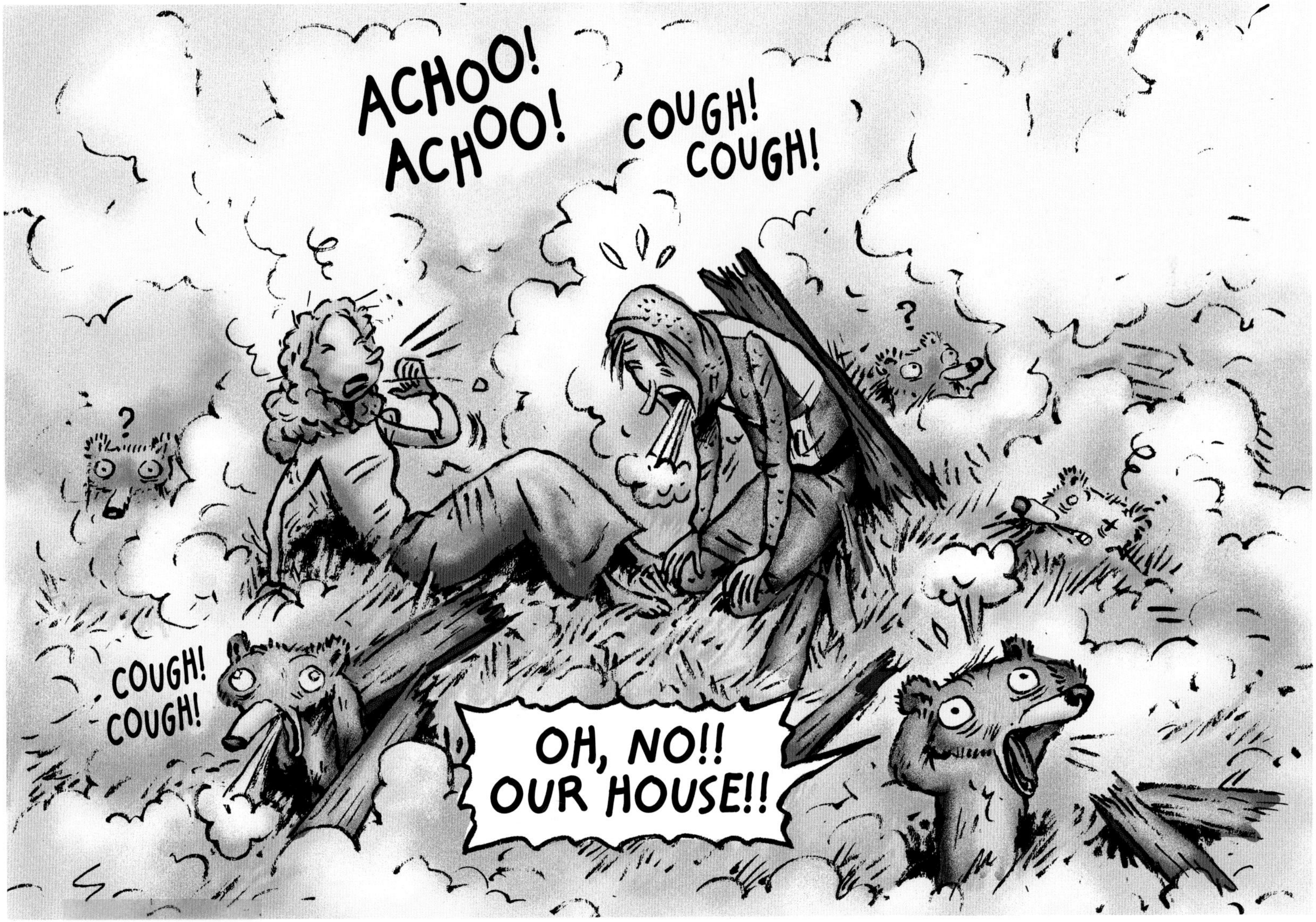
ACHOO!
ACHOO!
COUGH!
COUGH!
COUGH!
COUGH!
OH, NO!!
OUR HOUSE!!

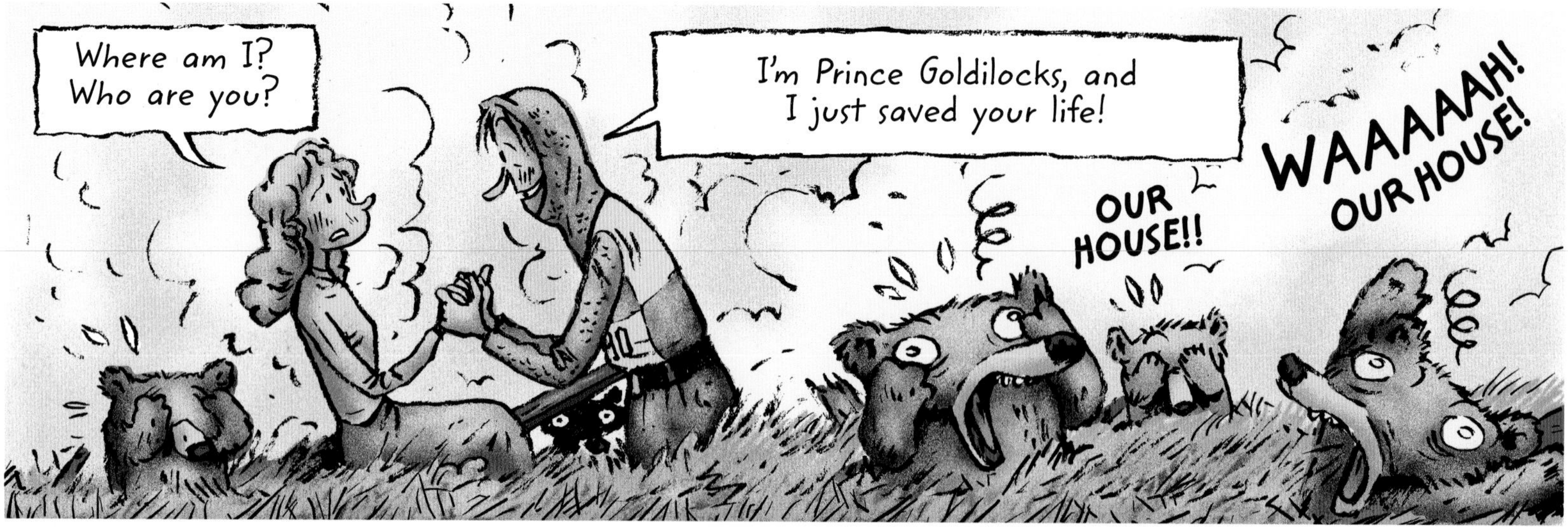
Where am I? Who are you?
I'm Prince Goldilocks, and I just saved your life!
OUR HOUSE!!
WAAAAAH! OUR HOUSE!

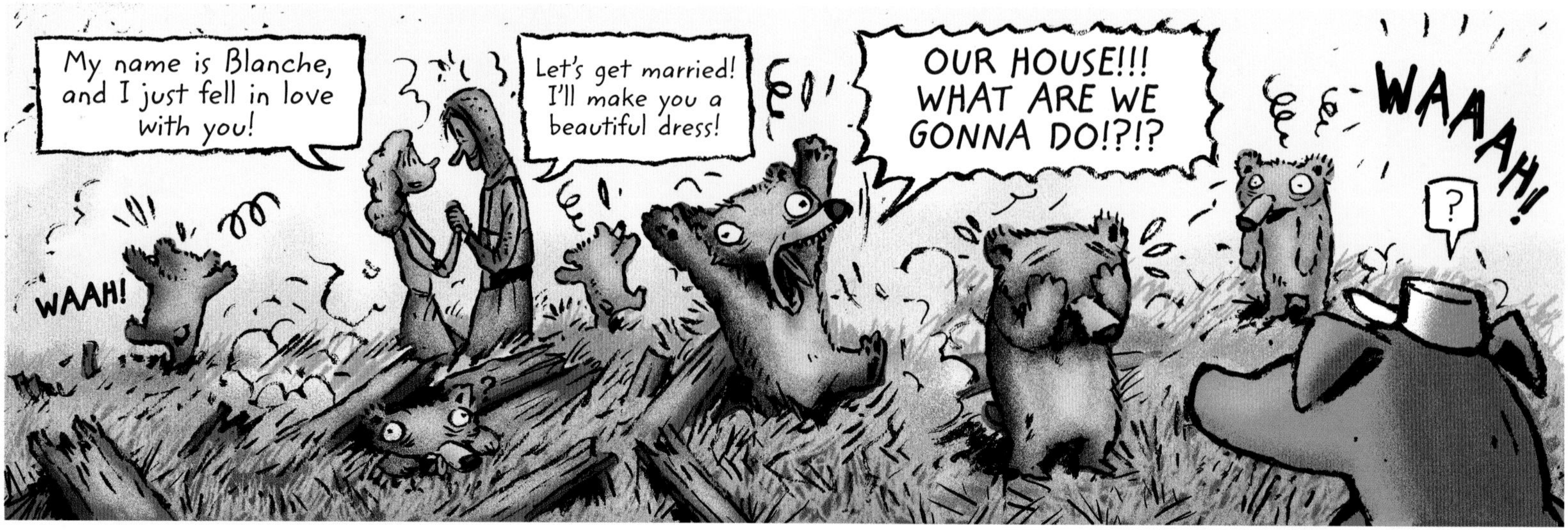
My name is Blanche, and I just fell in love with you!
Let's get married! I'll make you a beautiful dress!
OUR HOUSE!!! WHAT ARE WE GONNA DO!?!?
WAAAH!
WAAH!
?

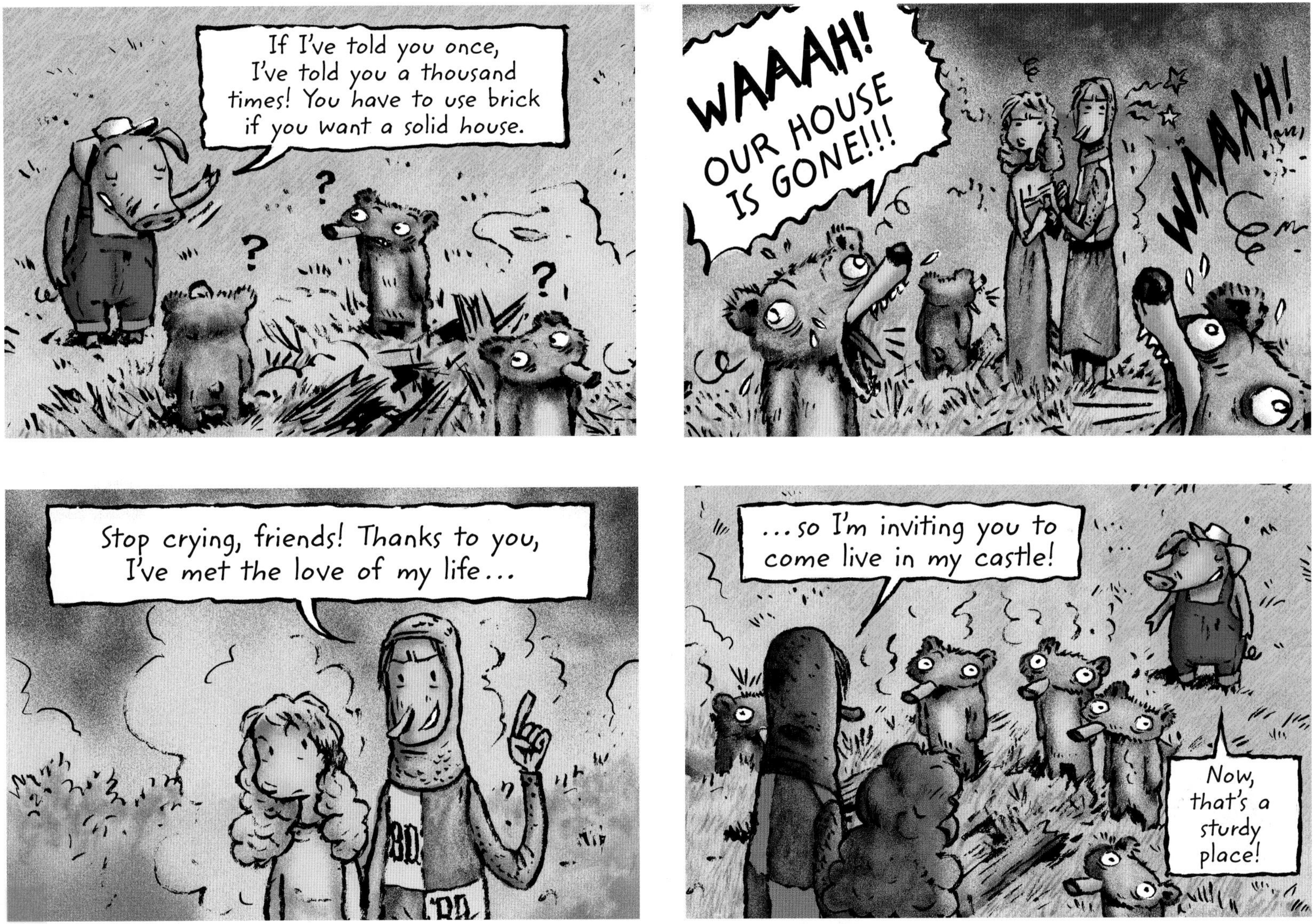
If I've told you once, I've told you a thousand times! You have to use brick if you want a solid house.
?
?
?
WAAAH! OUR HOUSE IS GONE!!!
WAAAH!
Stop crying, friends! Thanks to you, I've met the love of my life...
...so I'm inviting you to come live in my castle!
Now, that's a sturdy place!

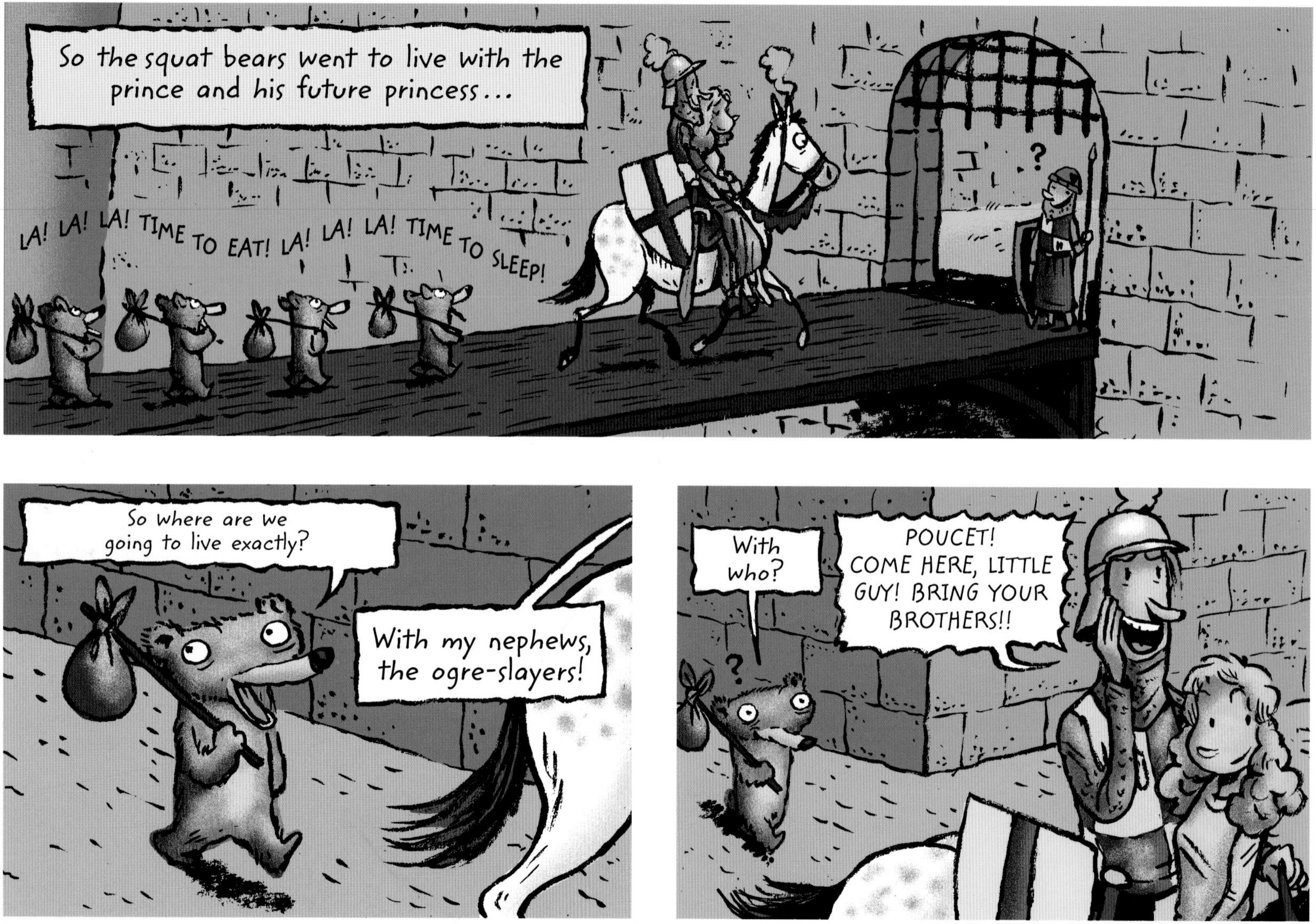
So the squat bears went to live with the prince and his future princess...
LA! LA! LA! TIME TO EAT! LA! LA! LA! TIME TO SLEEP!
?
So where are we going to live exactly?
With my nephews, the ogre-slayers!
With who?
?
POUCET! COME HERE, LITTLE GUY! BRING YOUR BROTHERS!!

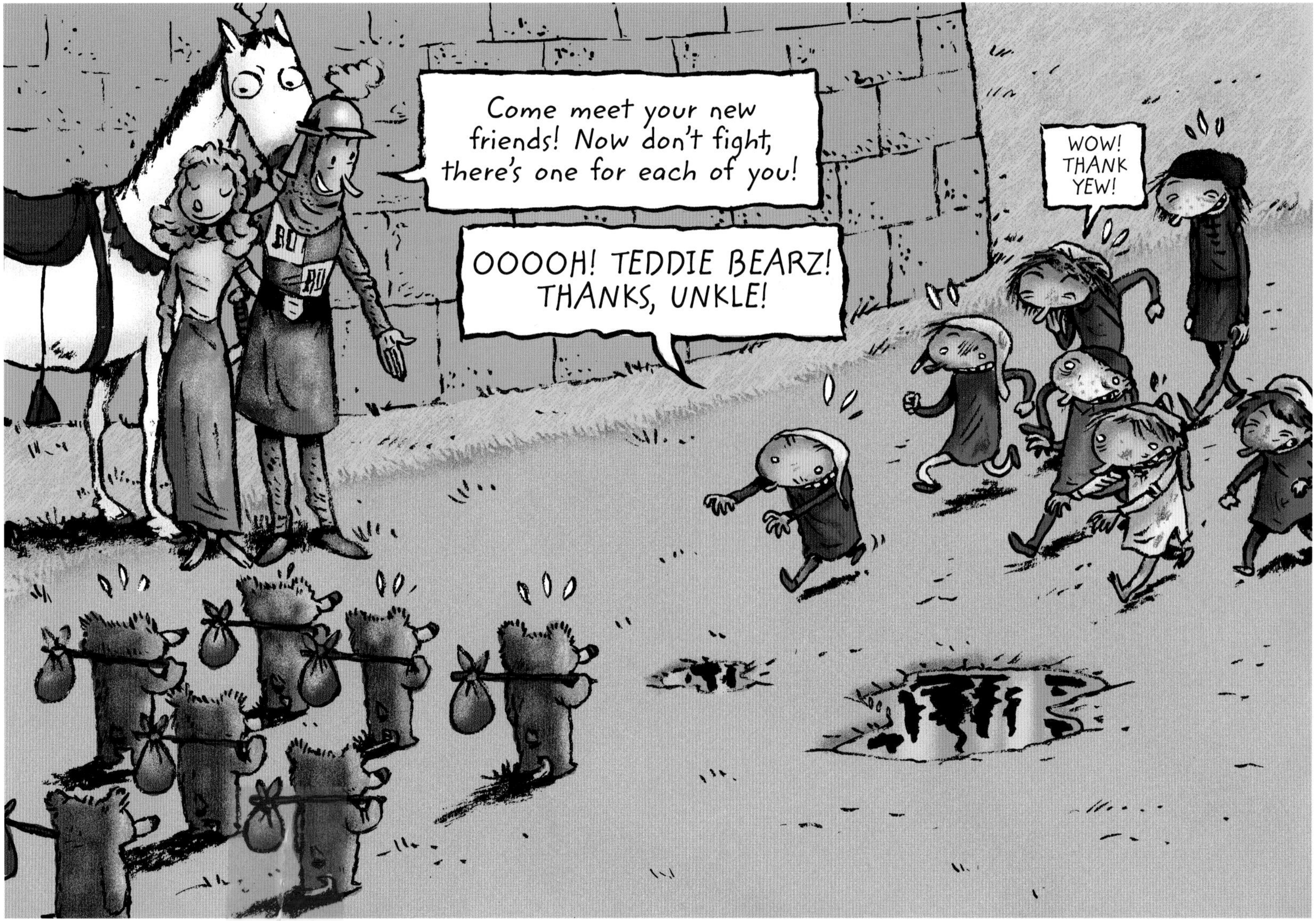
Come meet your new friends! Now don't fight, there's one for each of you!
OOOOH! TEDDIE BEARZ! THANKS, UNKLE!
WOW! THANK YEW!

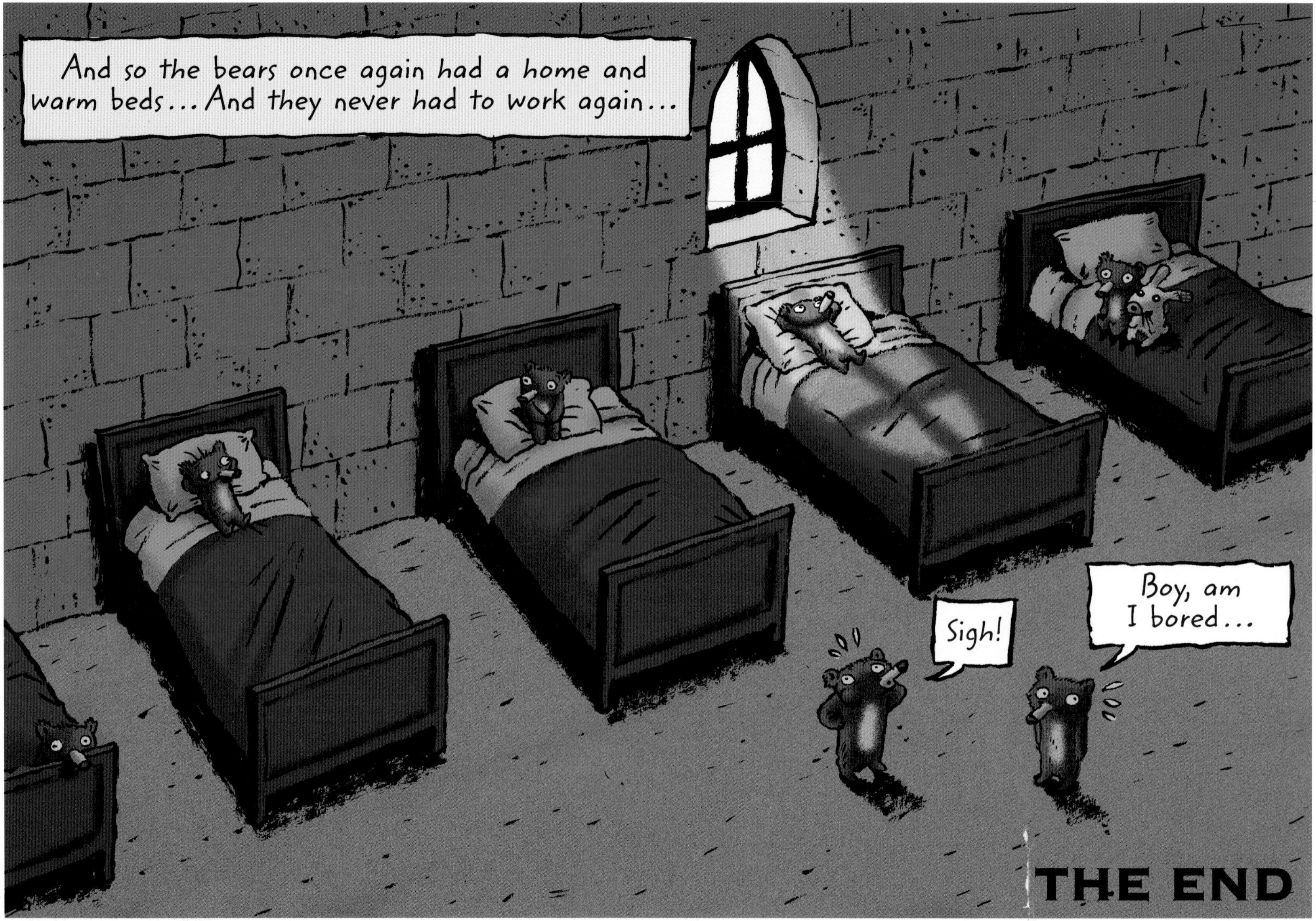
And so the bears once again had a home and warm beds... And they never had to work again...
Sigh!
Boy, am I bored...
THE END

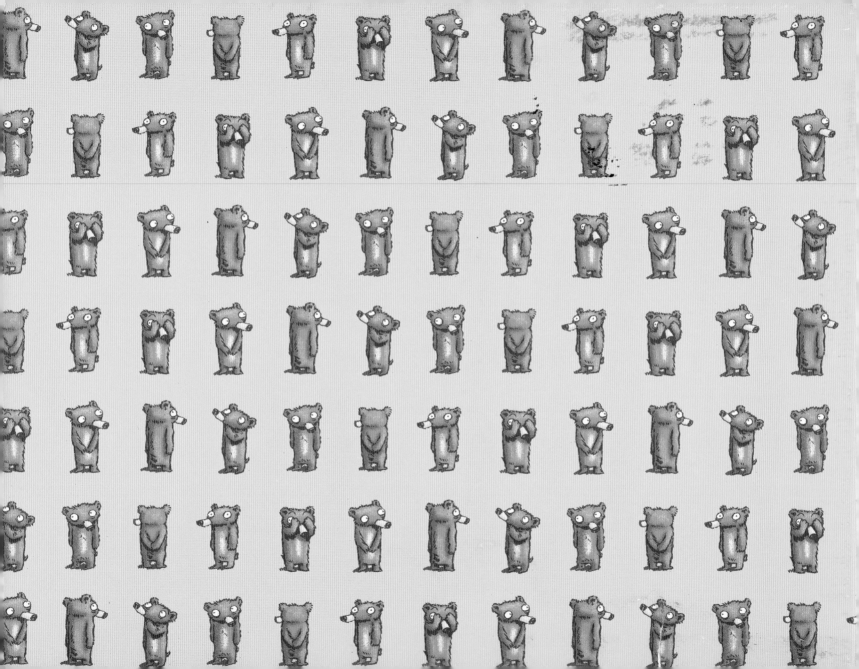